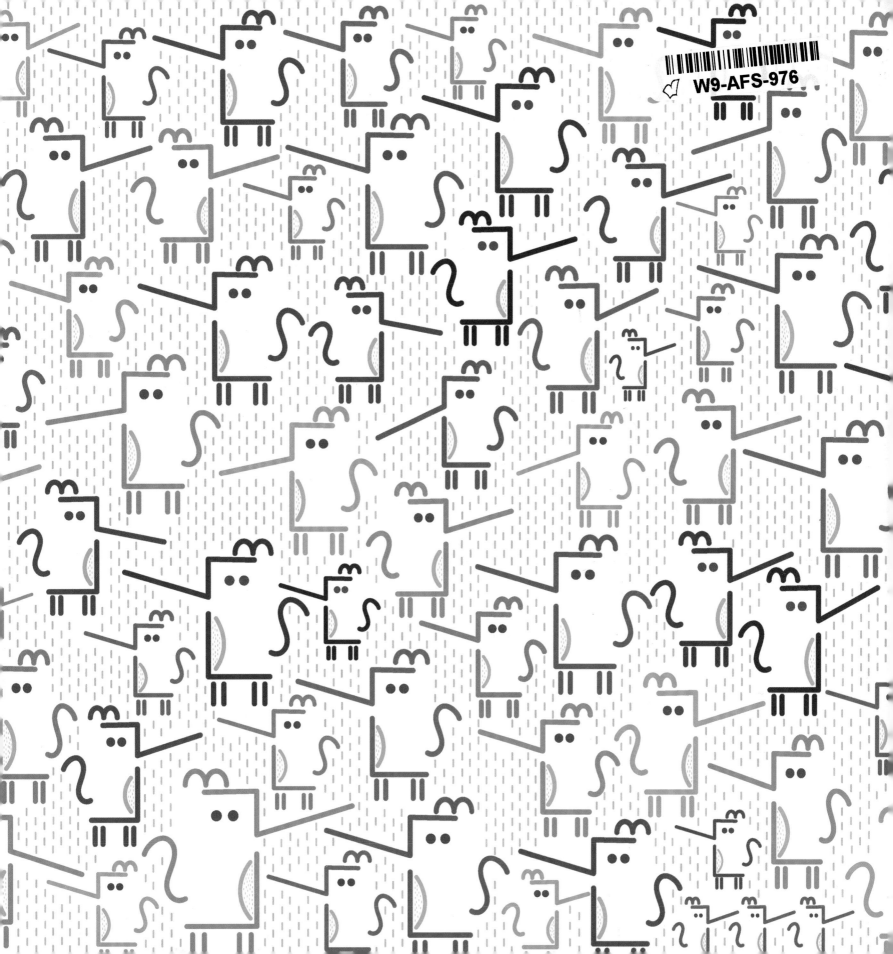

W9-AFS-976

For Eric,
I love to rediscover the world through the way you look at it.

Raquel

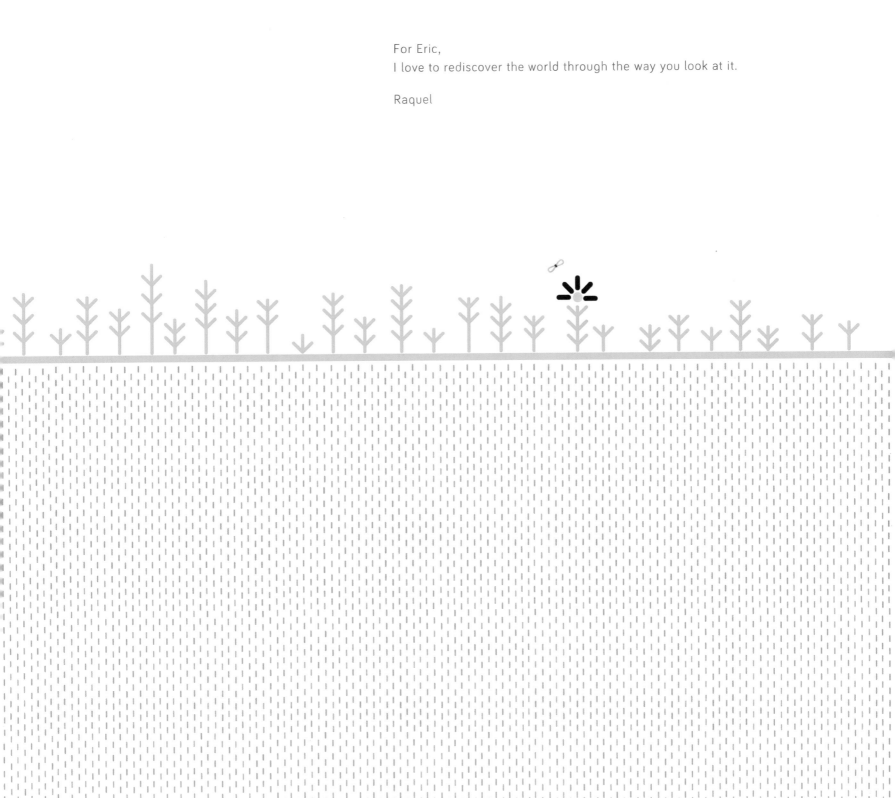

Reycraft Books
55 Fifth Avenue
New York, NY 10003

Reycraftbooks.com

Reycraft Books is a trade imprint and trademark of Newmark Learning, LLC.

© Tous sauf une, Balivernes Éditions, 2021
16 rue de la Doulline - 69340 Francheville - France
Translation rights arranged through Syllabes Agency, France

All rights reserved. No portion of this book may be reproduced, stored in a retrieval
system, or transmitted in any form or by any means, electronic, mechanical, photocopying,
recording, or otherwise, without written permission from the publisher.
For information regarding permission, please contact info@reycraftbooks.com.

Educators and Librarians: Our books may be purchased in bulk for promotional, educational,
or business use. Please contact sales@reycraftbooks.com.

This is a work of fiction. Names, characters, places, dialogue, and incidents described either
are the product of the author's imagination or are used fictitiously. Any resemblance to actual
persons, living or dead, is entirely coincidental.

Sale of this book without a front cover or jacket may be unauthorized. If this book is coverless, it
may have been reported to the publisher as "unsold or destroyed" and may have deprived
the author and publisher of payment.

Library of Congress Control Number: 2021914569

ISBN: 978-1-4788-7545-1

Printed in Dongguan, China. 8557/0721/18155

10 9 8 7 6 5 4 3 2 1

First Edition Hardcover published by Reycraft Books 2021.

Reycraft Books and Newmark Learning, LLC support diversity and the First Amendment,
and celebrate the right to read.

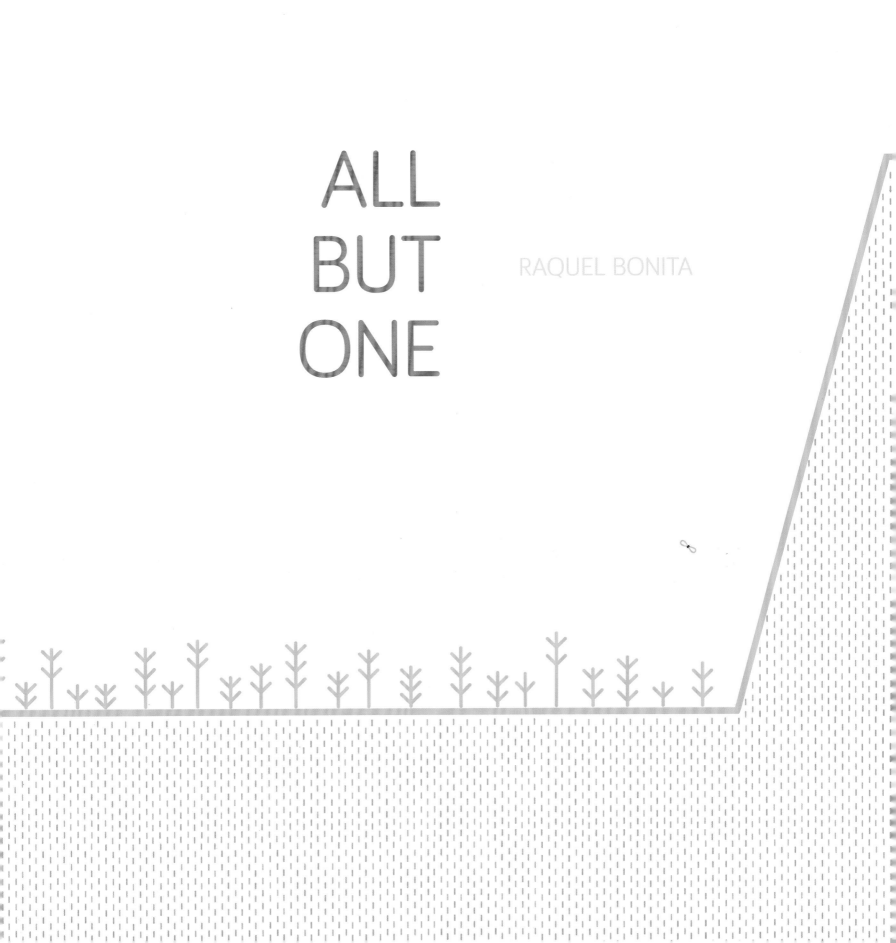

ALL
BUT
ONE

RAQUEL BONITA

All.

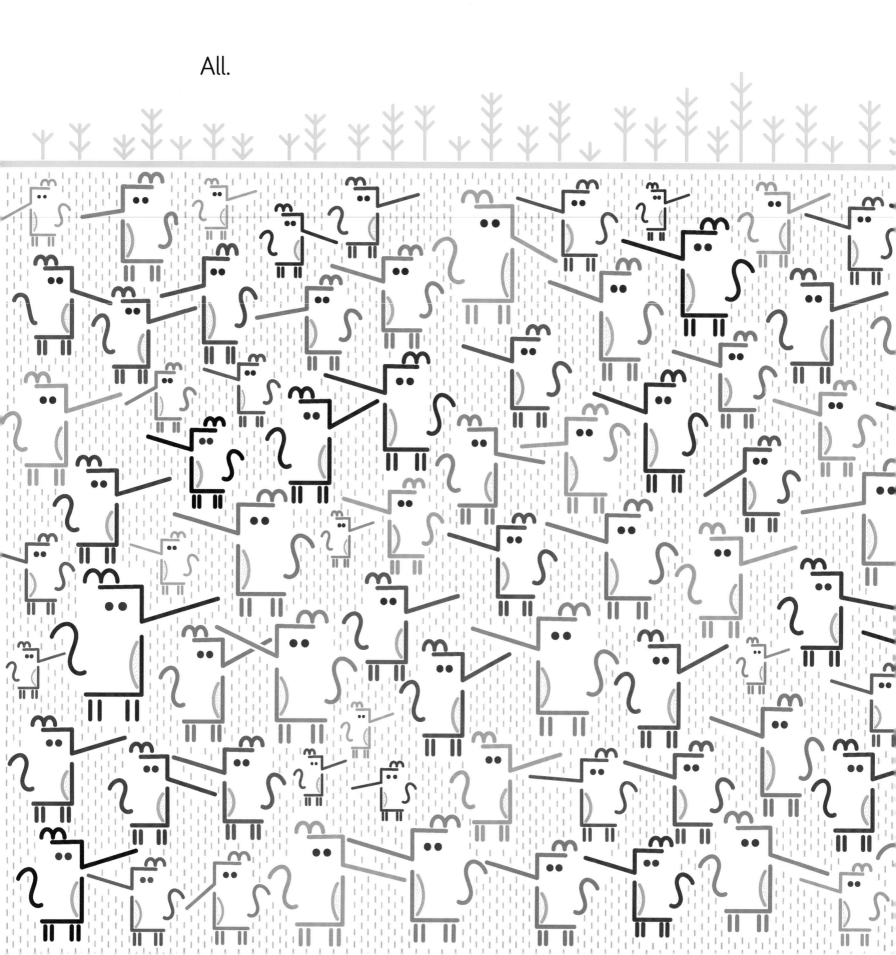

All but one.

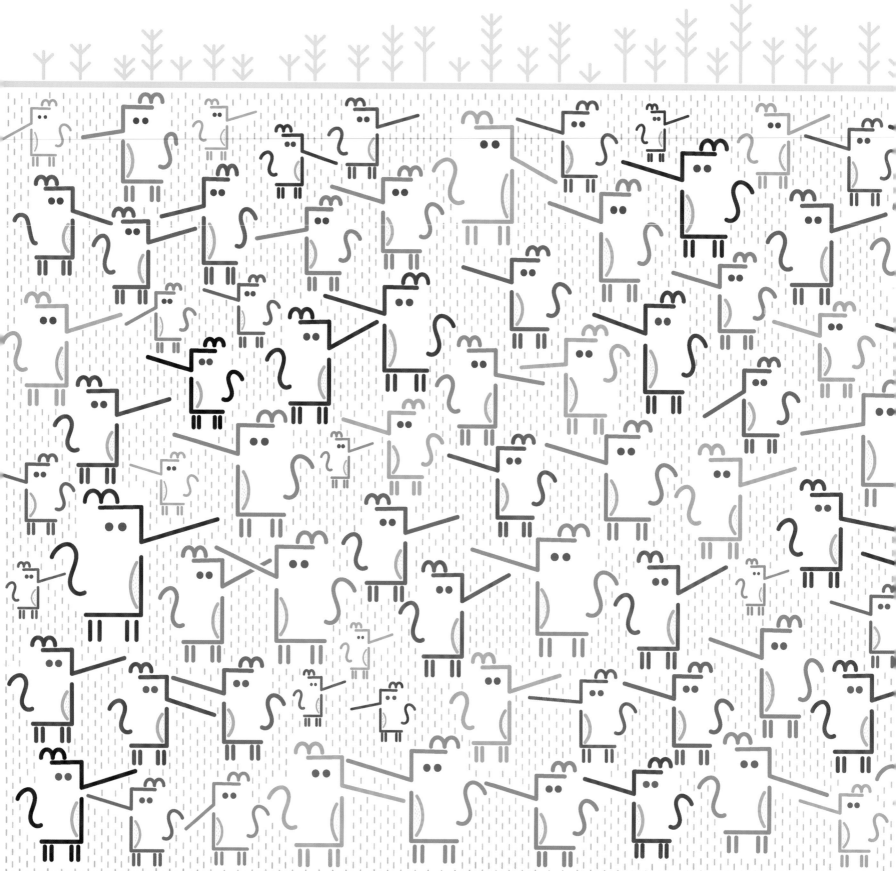

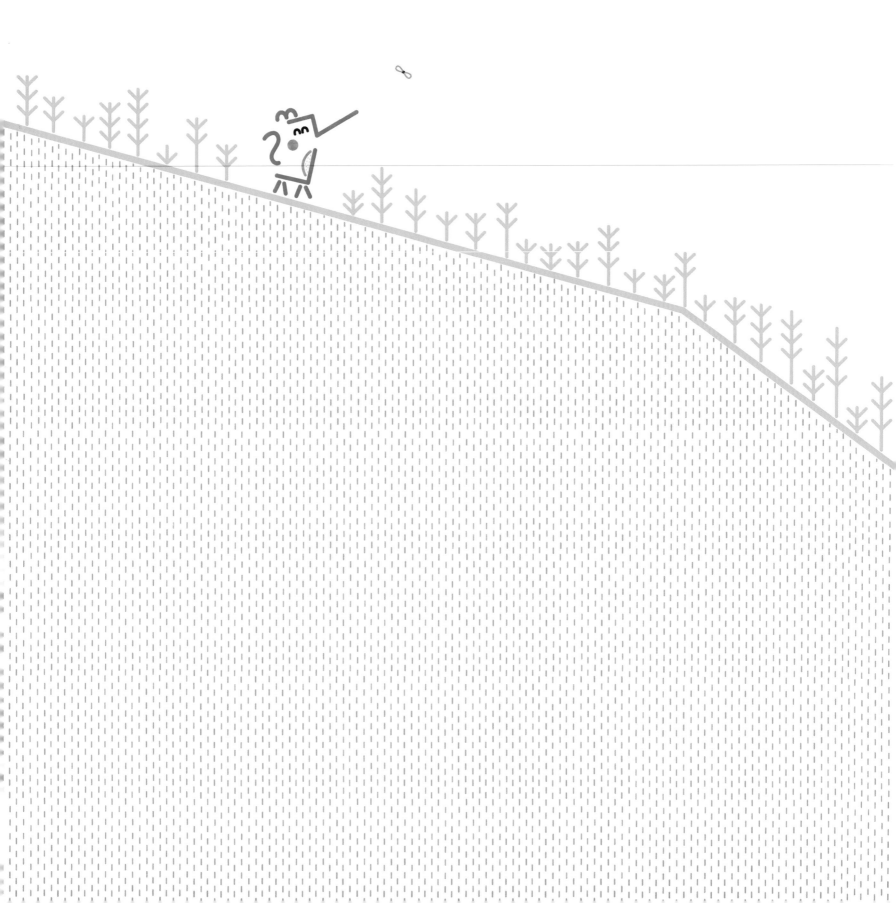

One.

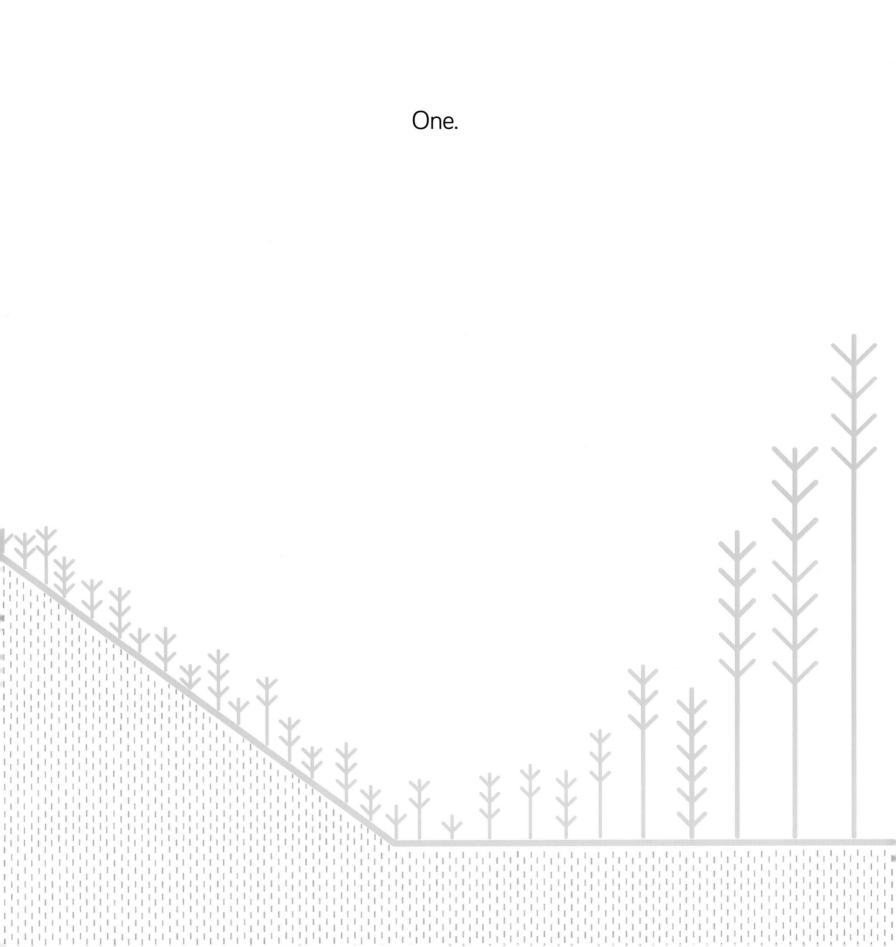

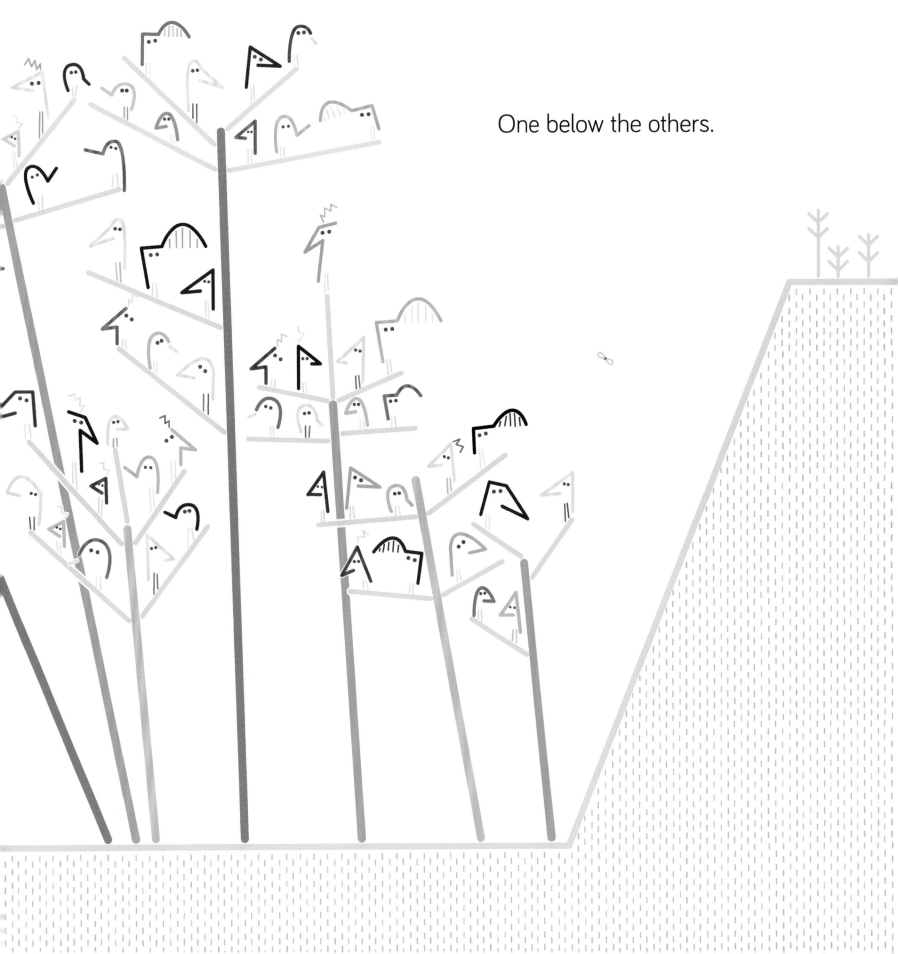

One below the others.

One above the others.

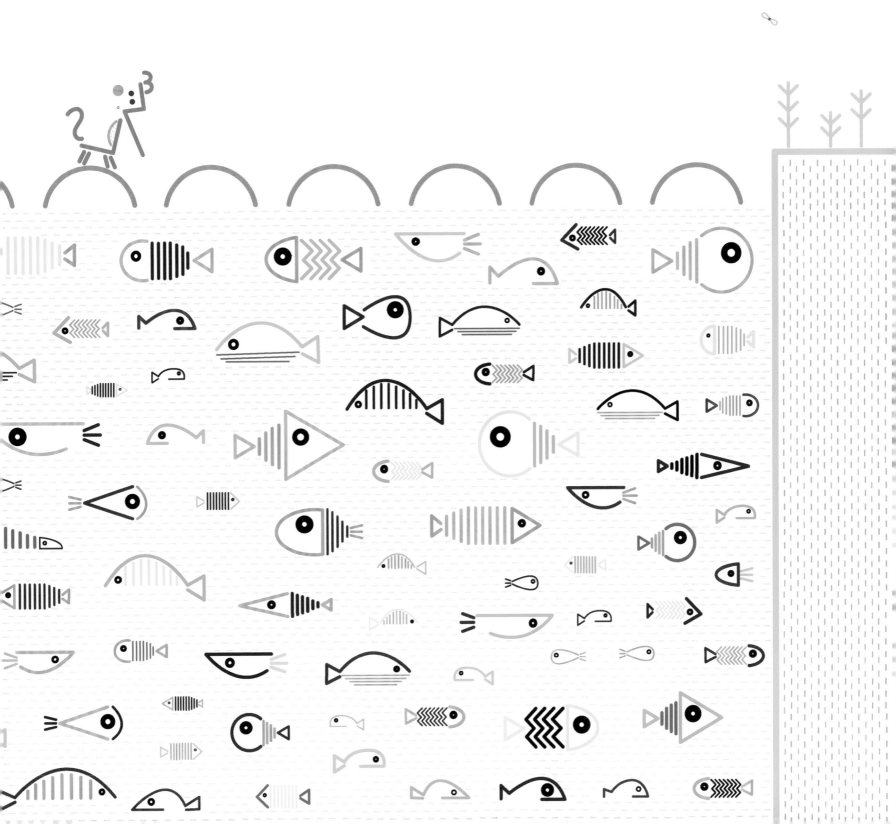

One among the others.

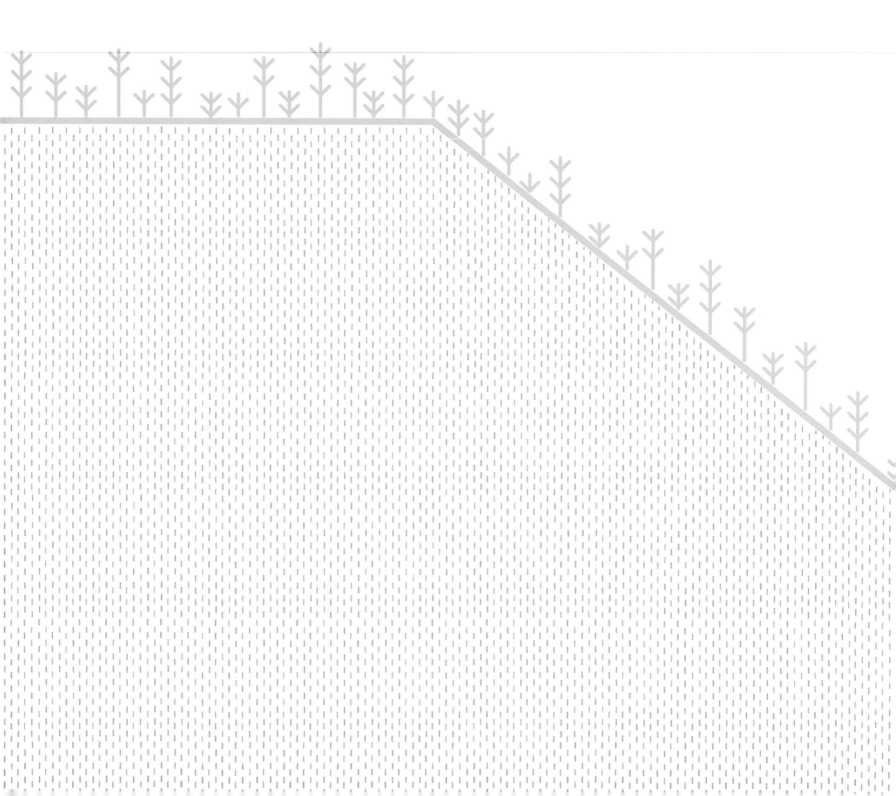

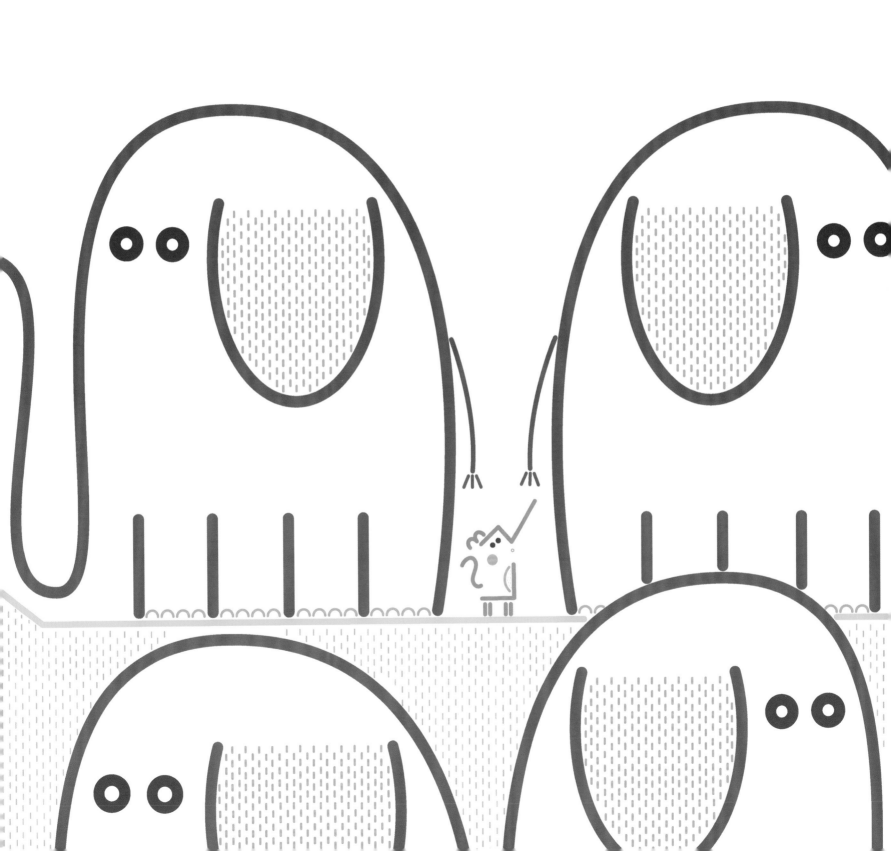

But the others are different.

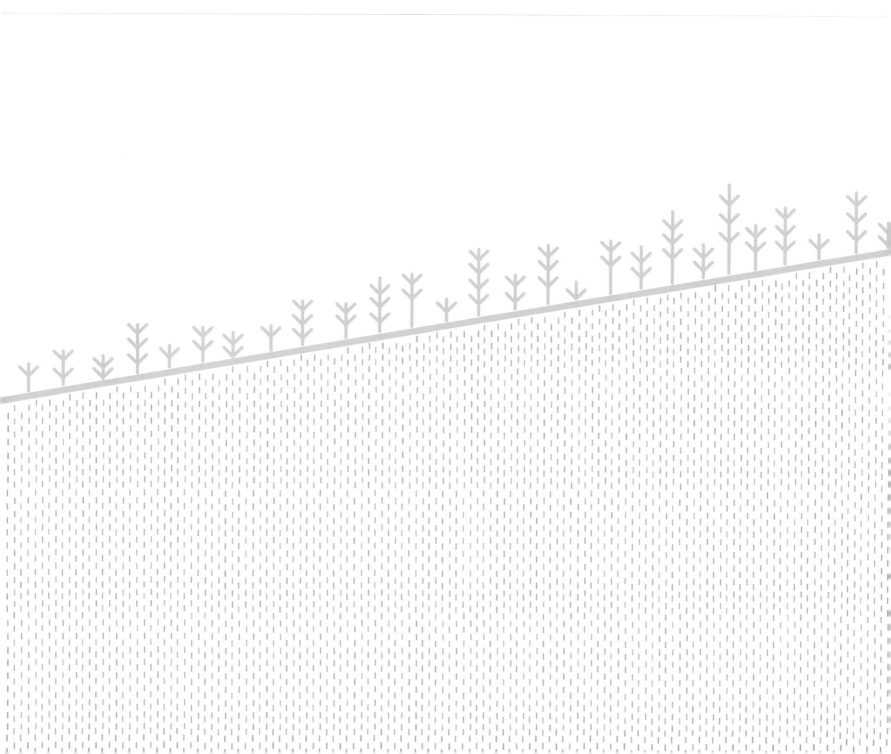

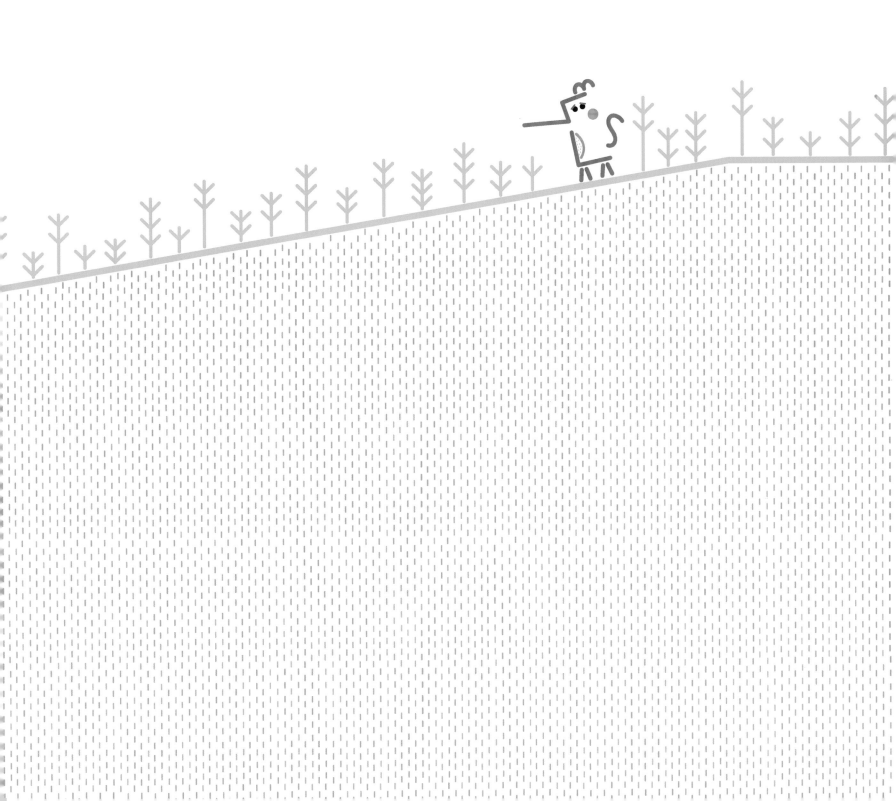

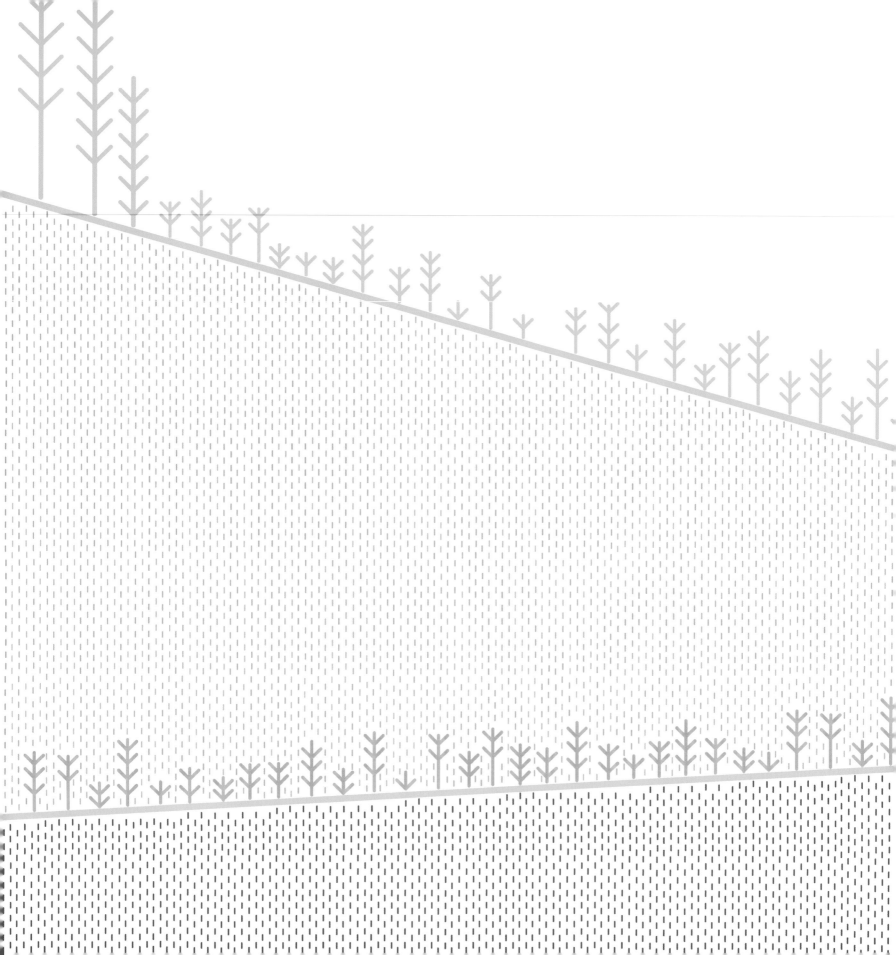

Just one. Alone.

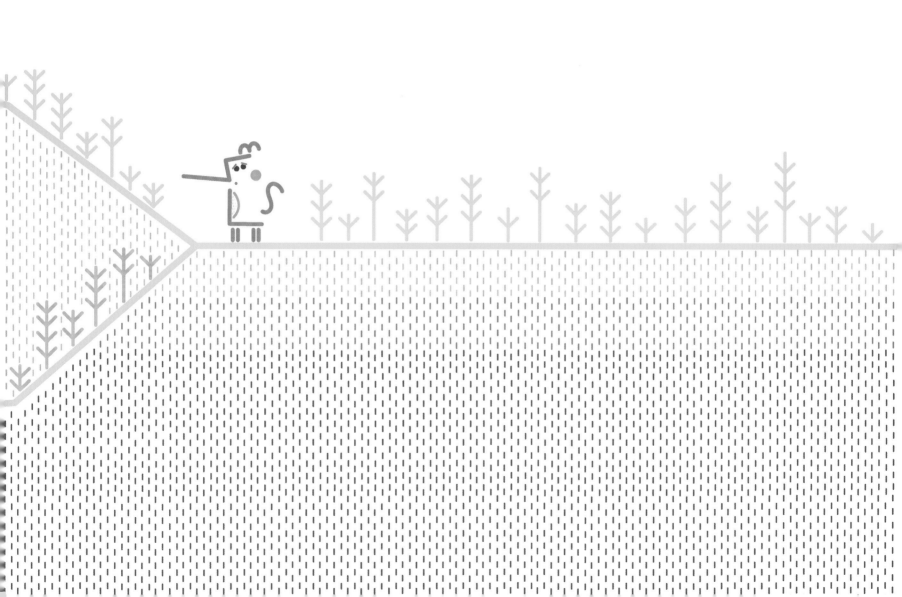

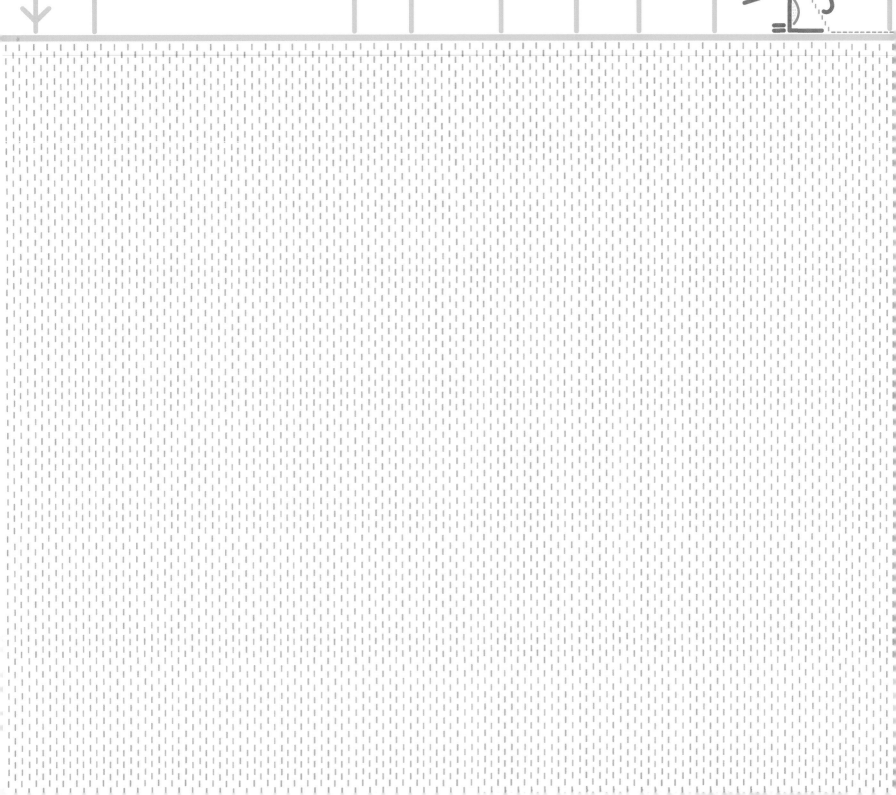

One!

One?

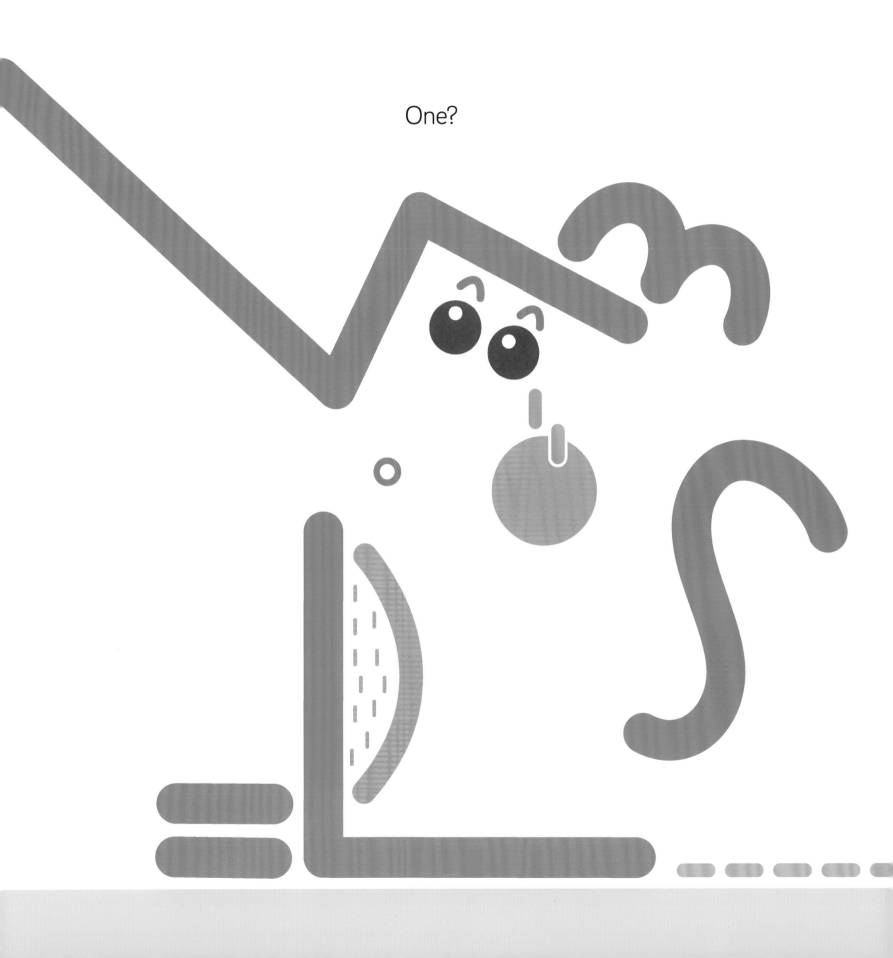

Two!

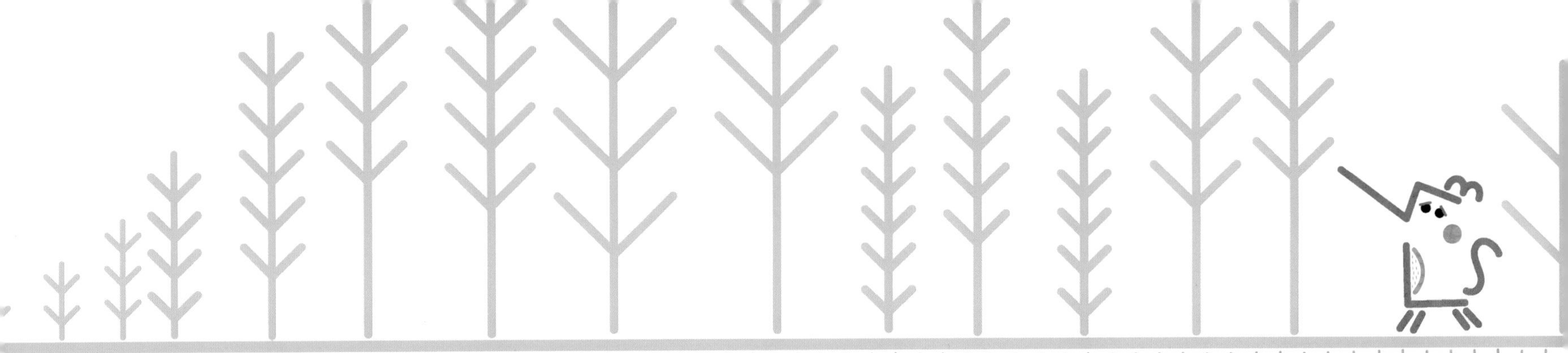

Three!

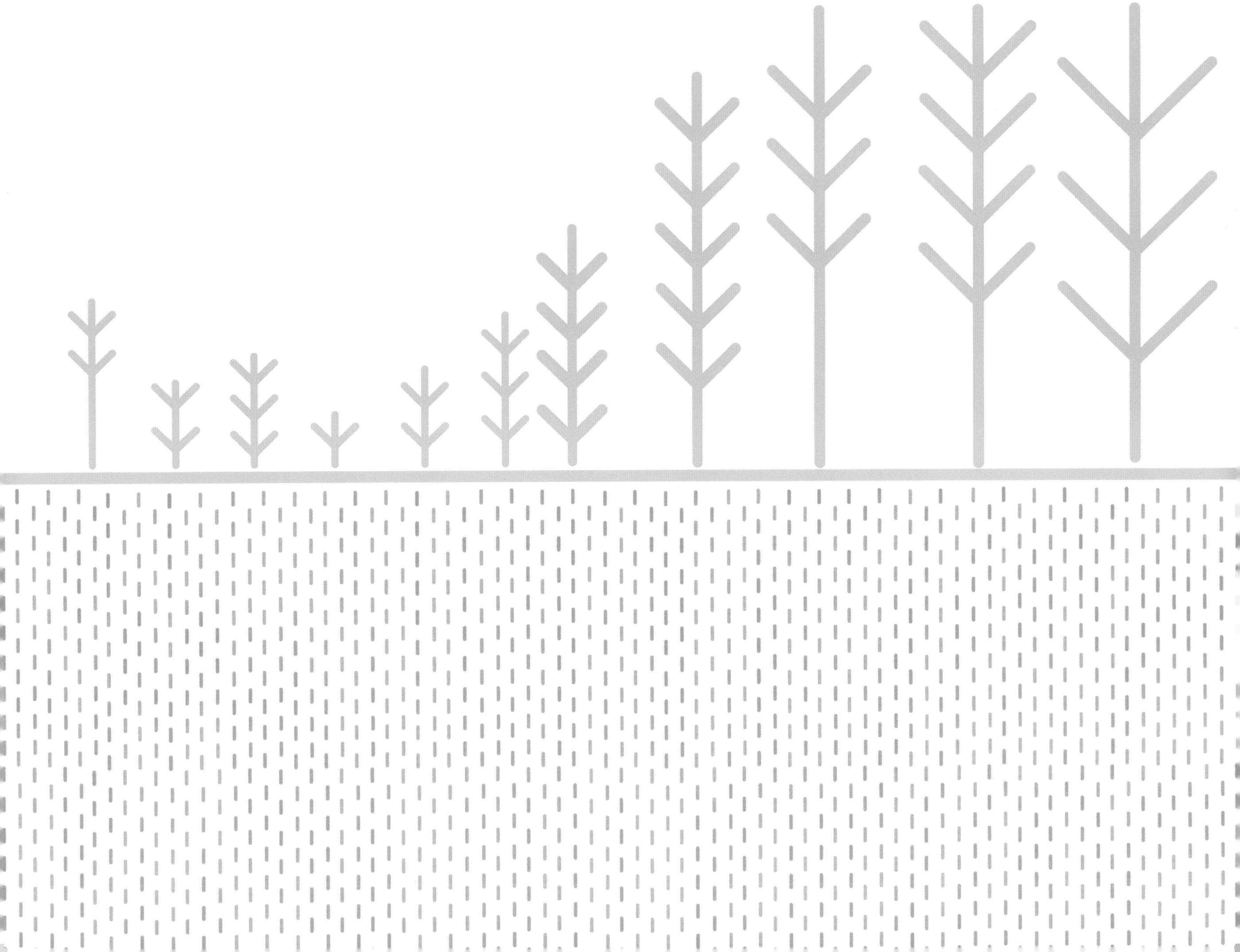

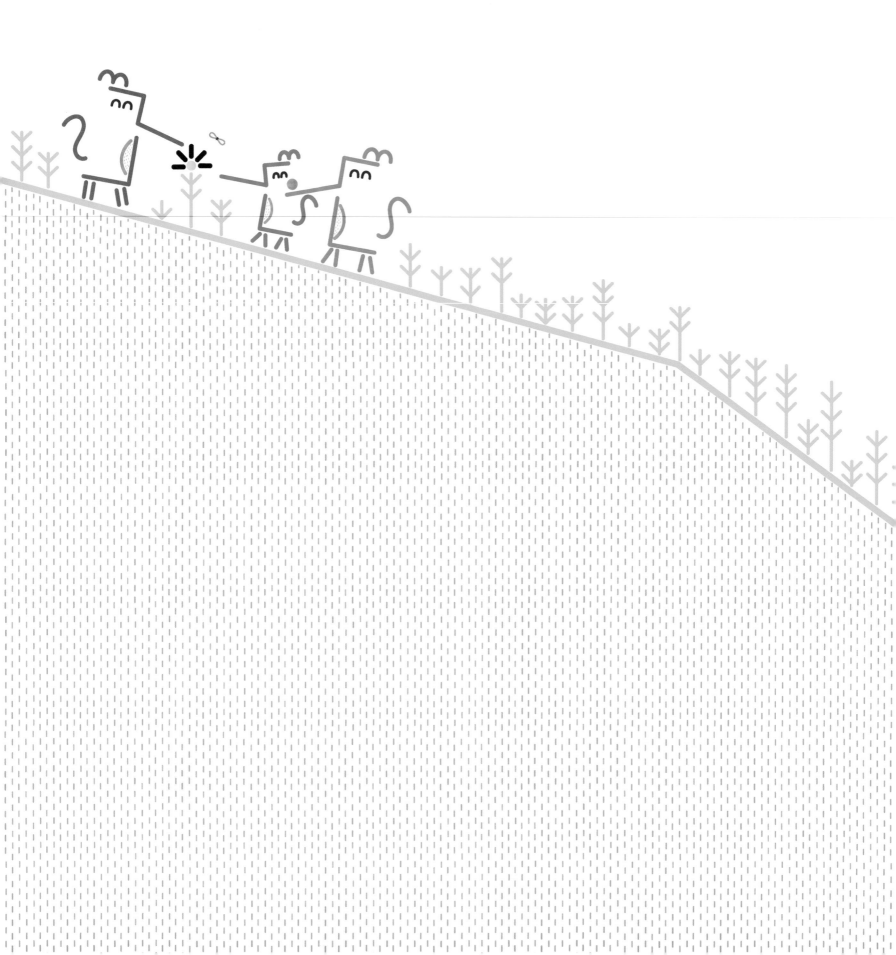

Together.

RAQUEL BONITA

 is an award-winning author and illustrator from northern Spain. In *All But One*, she wanted to capture the essence of animals using only a few lines. This book earned a Special Mention in the 2018 Golden Pinwheel Young Illustrators Competition.